Garfield's PET FORCE™

MENACE
OF THE
MUTANATOR

Produced by Creative Media Applications, Inc., and Paws Incorporated

Cover by Gary Barker, Mike Fentz, and Tom Howard
Graphics by Tom Howard and Jeff Wesley

ISBN 0-590-05945-9

12 11 10 9 8 7 6 5 4 3   8 9/9 0 1 2 3/0

Printed in the U.S.A.   40

First Scholastic printing, August 1998

Garfield's PET FORCE™

MENACE OF THE MUTANATOR

Created by
Jim Davis

Character development by
Mark Acey & Gary Barker

Written by
Michael Teitelbaum

Illustrated by
Gary Barker & Larry Fentz

SCHOLASTIC INC.
New York Toronto London Auckland Sydney

Introduction

When a group of lovable pets — Garfield, Odie, Arlene, Nermal, and Pooky — are transported to an alternate universe, they become a mighty superhero team known as . . . *Pet Force*!

Garzooka — Large and in charge, he is the fearless and famished leader of Pet Force. He's a ferocious feline with nerves of steel, a razor-sharp right claw, and the awesome ability to fire gamma-radiated hairballs (as well as deadly one-liners) from his mouth.

Odious — Although utterly clueless, he possesses incredible strength, ultra-slippery slobber, and a super-stretchy stun tongue. Onc zap of his lethal wet tongue causes a total mental meltdown in anyone he unleashes it upon.

Starlena — Sings a *purrfectly* pitched siren song ("the meow that wows!"). Anyone who hears her hypnotic song immediately falls into a trance — except Garzooka.

Abnermal — Has a body temperature of absolute zero; one touch of his icy paw freezes foes in their tracks. He can extend a nuke-proof force field to protect himself, as well as the other Pet Force members. His pester-power — more annoying than your little brother! — is one power that Garzooka could live without.

Compooky — Part-computer, part-teddy, this cyberbear extraordinaire is not only incredibly cute, but is also the mental giant of the team (not that big a deal).

Behold the mighty Pet Force! *Let the fur fly!*

1

The story so far ...

There are a great many universes parallel to our own. Each of these universes is very much like ours, but each one differs in some ways. For example, in our universe Jon Arbuckle is a nice but dim-witted pet owner. In the particular parallel universe that concerns our story, Jon is a nice but dim-witted emperor. In our universe, Garfield, Odie, Nermal, and Arlene are pets, and Pooky is a teddy bear. When these five friends travel into the parallel universe ruled by Emperor Jon, they become superpowered heroes.

In each universe there is a dimensional portal, a doorway that connects one world to the other. When danger strikes in Emperor Jon's universe, the emperor summons Garfield, Odie, Nermal, Arlene, and Pooky, who pass through the dimensional doorway from our universe into that of Emperor Jon.

In our universe, the doorway is the cover of issue #100 of the *Pet Force* comic book. When that framed comic book cover — which hangs on the wall in Jon Arbuckle's living room — begins to glow, the doorway to the other universe opens and the pets are pulled into the cover. In Emperor Jon's universe, the doorway is a large magic cauldron that belongs to the emperor's trusted friend and adviser, Sorcerer Binky. When the five friends arrive in Emperor Jon's universe, they emerge from this magic cauldron, and they have been transformed into the superpowered heroes of Pet Force. The same thing is true in reverse: When it is time for the five to go home, they pass through the cauldron and come back out of the comic book cover into their own universe.

The five furry friends are never missed by Garfield and Odie's owner, Jon Arbuckle, while they are in Emperor Jon's universe. Because of the difference in the way time moves in the two universes, Garfield and his friends could be away having an adventure in the parallel universe for days or weeks, while only seconds pass in our universe. The fact that Jon Arbuckle's brain runs a few minutes behind the rest of the world doesn't hurt, either!

When trouble arises in Emperor Jon's universe, it is usually caused by Vetvix, an evil veterinarian. Using evil spells and dark magic, Vetvix has vowed to conquer the universe and replace good Emperor Jon as its ruler. To help achieve her goal, Vetvix has created an army of mutant animals to serve her. Through her experiments, she has turned each animal into an extra-powerful and extra-evil warrior.

Vetvix's schemes to conquer Emperor Jon's universe would succeed if not for the power of Pet Force — those five furry defenders of justice who have stopped her again and again.

After Pet Force stopped Vetvix's most recent threat — K-Niner, the Dog of Doom (see Book #3 for details) — Emperor Jon tried to send the heroes back home to their own universe through a small computerized cauldron of Sorcerer Binky's.

But nothing happened!

Something was blocking the dimensional portal. The doorway to their universe would not open, and Pet Force was trapped in Emperor Jon's universe, unable to get home! Would they be stuck there forever? Would Garfield always remain Garzooka, never again to taste the gooey goodness of Earthly lasagna? Would Nermal be forced to always annoy others with the cosmic ability of Abnermal, rather than only the extremely annoying ability of his Earthly self? Could this be the end of Jon Arbuckle's lovable pets (and Garfield)? Well, what are you asking me for? Turn the page and find out!

2

Emperor Jon's universe . . .

The five members of Pet Force paced nervously around Emperor Jon's throne room. Each one stopped every so often and looked into the small cauldron that sat in the center of the room, then grumbled or snarled and resumed the pacing.

"I can't believe we're stuck here," whined Abnermal, his superfeline pester-power in rare form. He tried to shove Garzooka out of his way as he paced, but the equally cranky Pet Force leader stood his ground. "All the other times, it was zap into this universe, fight the bad guy, save the universe from unspeakable evil, then go home. Why can't we go home now?"

"As I explained to you earlier," began Compooky, trying to do everyone a favor by calming Abnermal down, "something is blocking the doorway between universes. I have been attempting to analyze the situation and find a solution using my supercomputer brain, but so far I have been unsuccessful."

"There's got to be a way!" exclaimed Garzooka, grabbing the edge of the cauldron and staring at the calm surface of the liquid inside. "I miss my favorite napping corner in Jon Arbuckle's living room."

"Are you kidding?" shot back Starlena. "You could nap hanging upside down in a moving roller coaster!"

"Well, there's one good thing about this," said Emperor Jon, trying to cheer everyone up. "At least things can't get any worse!"

Little did they know how wrong Emperor Jon was!

Our universe, Jon Arbuckle's backyard . . .

"I've got it!" called Jon Arbuckle. He turned his back to the volleyball net and started running at top speed, racing back to try to get to the ball that had just bounced off Odie's head. Jon dashed toward a hedge of low bushes that formed the border of his backyard. Diving for the ball, he crashed into the hedge headfirst, his orange sneakers waving in the air. The ball sailed over the hedge into the neighbor's yard.

Jon, Odie, Garfield, Arlene, Nermal, and Pooky had been playing a friendly game (for the most

6

part) of backyard volleyball when Odie had punched the ball over the hedge.

"I'm all right, guys!" shouted Jon. "Don't worry." He slowly pulled himself from the bushes and turned back toward the net, expecting to see Garfield, Odie, Arlene, Nermal, and Pooky. But when Jon turned around, his pets were gone. They had vanished, seemingly into thin air.

Because time moved differently in the two universes, only seconds had passed in Jon Arbuckle's universe since Garfield and the others had disappeared, while days had passed in Emperor Jon's universe — time enough for Pet Force to have had their K-Niner adventure and returned to the emperor's palace, where they now stood huddled around the cauldron.

Now Jon looked around his backyard. "Huh?" he said, using one of his favorite expressions. "Hey, guys!" he called out. "Guys? Where did you go?"

Jon ran around the backyard, calling out the names of his pets. He dashed from one corner of the yard to another, searching and shouting. Then he realized that the backyard was not that big. In fact, you could see all of it from where he was standing, and his pets were not in sight.

"Very funny, guys," he called out. "But you're playing the wrong game. We're playing volleyball, not hide-and-seek. Or maybe you're just trying to make me look like a fool!"

If Garfield had been there, he might have said something like, *Too late!* But Garfield was not in Jon's backyard. In fact, he was not even in Jon's universe!

"I get it!" said Jon, which if it were true would have been a first for him. "You guys didn't want to come outside in the first place, even though it's a beautiful spring afternoon. You probably all just ran back into the house while I was chasing the ball."

Jon ran into his house and began a frantic search for his pets. He checked the bedroom, the closets, and even the basement, but there was no sign of the pets. *This is really weird,* he thought. *We're not out of food or beds, so why would Garfield leave?* He checked the pantry, half expecting to find Garfield gnawing at a tuna can, but there was no sign of the fat cat or his friends. The house was empty.

Jon decided to take one last look around before getting really worried. He searched his living room, looking under the couch cushions, on top of the VCR, and under the coffee table.

Still nothing.

As he hunted around the living room, Jon failed to notice (so what else is new?) that Nermal's copy of the special embossed, gold foil, 3-D, holographic, glow-in-the-dark cover of the *Pet Force* comic, issue #100 — which hung on his wall in a frame — was beginning to glow. This very cover

was the doorway between our universe — Jon Arbuckle's universe — and the universe of Emperor Jon. And it was through this cover that Garfield and his friends traveled to the other universe.

"Well, that's it. I can't find them," said Jon. "I guess it's officially time to start worrying. Maybe I should call the police. I mean, no one just vanishes into thin air!"

At that very moment, the glowing comic book cover filled the room with a blinding flash of light.

ZAP! Jon vanished into thin air!

3

Emperor Jon's universe . . .

Jon felt himself tumbling through a long tunnel filled with brilliant white light. *Maybe I banged my head when I went diving for the ball,* he thought, trying to understand what was happening to him. *Maybe I'm unconscious and this is all some weird dream. When I open my eyes I'll be lying in my own backyard, looking up at my loving, concerned pets, who are worried sick about me. Yeah, that's probably it.*

Jon stopped tumbling and landed with a thud. He opened his eyes and saw that he was not lying on the soft green grass of his own backyard, but rather on a cold, hard linoleum floor. He looked up, but he didn't see his beloved pets. Instead he was surrounded by the five members of Pet Force.

Garzooka, Odious, Starlena, Abnermal, and Compooky all looked at each other in shock.

"It looks like Jon Arbuckle," Starlena whispered to Garzooka. "Could he really be here, in this universe?"

"Okay, it's time to wake up now," said Jon, getting to his feet. Then he pinched himself on the arm. "Ouch!" he yelped. "That hurt!"

"Yep, that's Jon all right!" said Garzooka.

"I guess I'm awake," said Jon. "But where am I? And how did I get here?" Jon looked around at the five furry friends who stood before him. "Don't I know you five?" he asked, looking the heroes up and down through squinted eyes. "You look very familiar."

Then it struck him. "Wow! It's *you guys!*" he shouted. "So *this* is where you went. Wherever *this* is. Great costumes, by the way. I love the whole superhero look, the padded muscles and everything, but Halloween isn't for a while yet."

Garzooka walked over and put his hand on Jon's shoulder. "It's kind of a long story, Jon," he said.

Jon leaped back in amazement. "Y-you t-talked," he stuttered. "Out loud. So that I can hear you! And you're standing on your hind legs. How is this possible?"

Jon kept backing away, thoroughly confused by the vision of the talking, muscle-bound Garfield who stood before him. After a few steps, Jon Arbuckle backed right into Emperor Jon.

"Oh, excuse me!" said Jon Arbuckle, spinning around to face the person he had bumped. "My mistake." He stared at the emperor — his exact double, down to the polyester clothes and flat-top sneakers. *What a good-looking guy!* he thought, looking at the emperor's royal robe and crown. *He looks just like me.*

It took a few seconds, as it always did with Jon. Then he realized that he was looking at his mirror image. "Hey!" he shouted. "How come you look just like me?"

"Please," said Emperor Jon, opening a plastic folding chair for Jon Arbuckle. "Sit down. Let me explain what's going on here." The emperor looked at Jon Arbuckle and thought, *Now* this *guy is a snappy dresser!*

Jon Arbuckle took a seat. *Nice chair!* he thought.

"This is a little complicated," began the emperor. "I'll try to take it one step at a time. You have come through a dimensional portal into a universe parallel to your own universe. Your pets came through the same portal earlier. When they passed through this doorway they became Pet Force, the superhero team you see before you — Garzooka, Odious, Starlena, Abnermal, and Compooky. Each of them gained a different body and incredible super powers."

"Not to mention really cool costumes," interrupted Jon.

"As Pet Force they fight for freedom and justice," continued the emperor. "They are the brave defenders of this universe and protectors of my throne."

"Who are you?" asked Jon Arbuckle. "Besides a guy who looks exactly like me and wears a robe and a crown?"

"I am Emperor Jon," replied the emperor, bowing. As he bent over, the seam in the backside of his pants split open. "I've definitely got to speak to the royal tailor about these pants." Then, refocusing his attention on Jon Arbuckle, he went on. "I am the ruler of this universe, and as ruler, I welcome you. Now, is there anything about this you don't understand?"

"Just the last part," replied Jon Arbuckle.

"Which part is that?" asked the emperor.

"The part after you said, 'This is a little complicated,'" replied Jon Arbuckle. It was all a bit much to understand for a guy who got confused watching reruns of *The Brady Bunch*.

The five members of Pet Force walked over to Jon Arbuckle. They were still shocked from seeing him in the emperor's universe. "How did you get here?" asked Garzooka.

"I have no idea," replied Jon.

Well, some things are the same no matter what universe you're in, thought Garzooka.

"We were playing volleyball," said Jon. "Then I dove for a ball, and when I got up you guys were gone. I searched the house and then suddenly I was here."

"Excuse me," said Compooky, who was hovering above the ground as usual.

"Pooky?" said Jon. "What's with the TV set on your head?"

"I'll explain in a moment," replied Compooky.

"But first, please tell me, what is the last room you remember being in?"

"The living room," replied Jon.

"The comic book cover!" exclaimed Abnermal.

"Precisely," said Compooky. "You see, the cover to *Pet Force* issue #100, which hangs in your living room, is a doorway out of your universe and into this one. We were actually trying to go home when you appeared here. Somehow, we were prevented from returning to your universe, and you were accidentally brought into this one."

"You mean that comic book on the wall is not a comic book, it's a door?" asked Jon, shaking his head. "Dimensional portals, comic book doorways, pets with big muscles, capes, and super powers, talking teddy bears . . . I think I want to just go home and reorganize my pot holders again. That I can handle."

Abnermal ran over to Jon Arbuckle. "Check out our cool powers!" he exclaimed. "Watch this!" He raised his arms, ready to fire a freeze blast.

"Why don't you let Garzooka go first?" suggested Starlena.

"Thanks," said Garzooka, stepping forward and shoving Abnermal out of the way.

"Age before beauty," Starlena whispered. Abnermal fell over, roaring with laughter.

Garzooka gave Starlena a nasty look, then fired a gamma-radiated hairball just inches over her head. The glowing glob of gunk hit the stone wall of the throne room with a *splat*, then burned a hole through the wall.

"Wow!" exclaimed Jon Arbuckle. "I've seen you cough up some pretty gnarly hairballs as Garfield, but even the worst one couldn't melt stone!"

Unlike your breath, thought Garzooka, deciding to keep the comment to himself.

"My turn!" announced Abnermal, stepping up to Jon and encasing him in a block of ice with his freeze-power.

"But I haven't shown off my strength or my razor-sharp right claw yet!" complained Garzooka, slamming Abnermal into a wall. The Pet Force leader flexed his right hand and his razor-sharp claw popped out, glinting menacingly in the light. With a few swift strokes, Garzooka sliced the ice off Jon, who sat in his folding chair, shivering.

"Sorry about Abnermal," said Garzooka. "His ability to pester has grown to cosmic proportions in this universe. Now, let me show you my unbelievable strength."

Garzooka dashed out of the palace. He planted his feet firmly at the base of the tall stone structure, then grabbed its foundation with his powerful hands. Straining his muscles, Garzooka lifted the entire palace up into the air.

Inside the throne room, Jon Arbuckle's chair went scooting across the linoleum floor, from one side of the room to the other, as the palace swayed in midair. Then Garzooka put the palace back down and dashed up the stairs to his friends.

"Wow! Now that's what I call strong!" exclaimed Jon.

"My turn! My turn!" yelled Abnermal once again. This time, when Garzooka went to slug him, Abnermal put up his force field in time to block the blow. Garzooka's hand bounced right off the invisible shield.

"That's a neat trick," said Jon. "The force field would come in handy when I'm walking through the park." Jon looked up and pointed. "You know pigeons. They love me. It's like I have a target painted on the top of my head."

Emperor Jon came over and looked at the top of Jon Arbuckle's head. "I don't see any target," said the emperor.

"I can see that you two are going to get along great," said Garzooka.

Starlena demonstrated her power next. "My siren song will put you into a trance," she explained. "Don't be afraid. It won't last for long."

Starlena sang out with the meow that wows, and everyone except Garzooka — who was immune to her power — fell into a trance.

When the trance wore off, Jon Arbuckle opened his eyes and yawned. "I just had the weirdest dream," he told the others. "I was pulled through the cover of a comic book into a parallel universe, and all my pets had big muscles and — oh. It wasn't a dream."

"I'm afraid not," said the emperor.

Odious trotted over to Jon Arbuckle and drooled on his foot.

"That's a nice super power," said Jon, trying to be polite.

"He's actually got incredible strength," explained Starlena. "Go ahead, Odious. Show him."

Odious jogged out of the throne room. He tried to imitate Garzooka's feat of lifting the palace off the ground, only he got confused and ran to the roof instead. He grabbed the edge of the roof and yanked with all his might. Two chunks of stone broke off, and with one in each hand, Odious went tumbling over the edge of the roof, crashing to the ground below.

Odious returned to the throne room a few minutes later and slobbered on Jon's other foot. Then he licked Jon's face, forgetting all about his super-stretchy stun tongue. Jon passed out and fell off his chair. Pet Force rushed to his side, and within a few minutes Jon had been revived.

"Sorry about that," Starlena apologized. "I didn't mention Odious's super-stretchy stun tongue."

"Wow," said Jon, sitting back in his chair. "That tongue packs quite a wallop. When he licks me in our universe, the most I have to worry about is taking a shower and putting my clothes in the dryer."

"He doesn't know his own strength," said Abnermal.

"Or much of anything else," muttered Garzooka.

"What about you, Pooky?" asked Jon. "What's your super power?"

"It's *Com*pooky in this universe," replied the cyberbear extraordinaire. "I'm a hyper-intelligent supercomputer."

"Wow!" Jon said for about the tenth time that day. "I'll bet you could *really* help me reorganize my pot holders!"

"You'll never even *see* those precious pot holders again if we don't figure out some way to get back home!" exclaimed Garzooka.

Emperor Jon brought his small computerized cauldron over to Jon Arbuckle. "What *I* don't understand —" he began.

Uh-oh! thought Garzooka. *We could be here all week!*

"— is why Pet Force couldn't return home through this cauldron — which I used to bring them here in the first place," continued the emperor. "Of course, I'd also like to know why you got pulled through into my universe. I will now try to send you back home using this cauldron."

"Do I have to click my heels together three times?" asked Jon Arbuckle.

"I don't think so," replied the emperor. He pressed a few buttons on the side of the tiny cauldron. Everyone stared down at the thick brown liquid in the cauldron, waiting for something to happen. Nothing did.

"Maybe the problem is with this cauldron that Sorcerer Binky gave me," said Emperor Jon, whacking the small tub on its side.

"Perhaps you should contact the sorcerer and have him bring his full-sized cauldron over," suggested Starlena. "Maybe he can send us all home that way."

The emperor summoned Sorcerer Binky, who soon arrived at the palace, dragging his large cast-iron cauldron behind him.

"Oh, boy! This thing is heavy!" complained the sorcerer as he placed the cauldron in the middle of the throne room. "I can't believe I had to drag this thing over here again! That's why I gave you the small computerized cauldron in the first place: so I wouldn't have to drag this thing all the way — whoa!"

Sorcerer Binky had turned around and spotted Jon Arbuckle. Then he looked back at the emperor. "I must have put a few too many lizard tongues into my stew last night. I think I'm seeing double!"

"Binky the Clown!" exclaimed Jon Arbuckle. "What's a nice clown like you doing in a universe like this?" Jon giggled at his own joke. He was the only one who did. Garzooka explained to Jon that in this universe, Binky was a sorcerer, not a clown.

The emperor filled Sorcerer Binky in on Jon Arbuckle's arrival and their problems in sending him and Pet Force back home. Then the sorcerer poured a sackful of ingredients into his cauldron and stirred. The magic brew began to bubble.

"It's working!" exclaimed Emperor Jon.

Then, just as quickly as it had started, the bubbling stopped.

"It's no use," said Sorcerer Binky. "The doorway between universes seems blocked, clogged. It's as if someone else has taken control of the cauldron's transporting power."

Suddenly a small whirlpool began spinning on the surface of Binky's magic brew. The brew swirled faster and faster, like a tornado, and grew larger and larger. The intense force of the twister pulled the five members of Pet Force toward the swirling opening in the cauldron.

"What's going on here?" yelled Abnermal.

"It's too strong!" groaned Starlena as she desperately fought to keep from being sucked into the cauldron. "I can't fight it!"

Sorcerer Binky chanted a magic spell right at the cauldron. *"Tuna melt with sliced tomato, stop this spinning dark tornado!"*

A thick, gooey tuna melt sandwich dropped from the air, splattering all over the sorcerer's pointy hat. The tornado, however, kept right on spinning.

"My magic is having no effect!" shouted Binky. "This magic tornado is too powerful!"

In a flash, Starlena was pulled into the spinning tornado, disappearing into the cauldron. Abnermal and Compooky followed. They were powerless against the titanic force of the twister and were swallowed up by the cauldron as well.

Odious used his great strength to resist the pull, but within a few seconds he, too, disappeared into the swirling opening.

Garzooka was next. His body was pulled halfway into the whirlpool. Only his head and arms stuck out as he struggled against the terrible tornado!

4

G arzooka gripped the sides of the cauldron with his powerful hands and pushed with all his strength.

"What's happening?" shouted Jon Arbuckle, overwhelmed by what he was seeing. Jon was a man who could be stunned by finding two socks that matched in the same drawer. This scene was almost too much to take.

"Four members of Pet Force were just sucked into the cauldron and disappeared," replied Emperor Jon. "Garzooka is now struggling to keep from being sucked in himself."

Boy, this guy is really smart! thought Jon Arbuckle, attempting to understand the emperor's explanation.

Garzooka's face dripped with sweat, which rolled down his cheek and mixed with a small piece of scrambled egg left over from breakfast. He was losing the battle with the tornado, slowly slipping into the cauldron. In a final desperate move, Garzooka fired a gamma-radiated hairball into the swirling storm.

The radioactive hairball shot into the center of the whirlpool and exploded. The force of the blast threw Garzooka free from the cauldron storm. He tumbled to the throne room floor. Then, just as quickly as it had opened, the swirling hole closed. The liquid in the cauldron was once again calm.

Which was more than could be said for the two Jons!

Emperor Jon and Jon Arbuckle rushed to Garzooka's side. "Garzooka!" exclaimed the emperor, helping the hero to his feet. "Are you all right?"

"Garfield-in-a-weird-superhero-costume, are you all right?" asked Jon Arbuckle.

"I'm fine," puffed Garzooka, out of breath. "A bit worn-out from my struggle, but it's nothing that a large lunch and a long nap couldn't fix."

"I'm afraid there's no time for that, Garzooka," said the emperor grimly. "Someone has definitely gained control of the cauldron's magic transporting power. That explains why you and your Pet Force teammates couldn't go back to your own universe." The emperor turned to Jon Arbuckle. "It must also be why you accidentally got pulled into this universe."

"Could you explain that part after you said, 'This is a little complicated' to me again?" asked Jon Arbuckle, still astonished by the events of the past few minutes.

Emperor Jon ignored Jon Arbuckle, but he was secretly relieved that there was someone in some universe who was actually lamer than he was.

"Now Starlena, Odious, Abnermal, and Compooky have been kidnapped," said Emperor Jon. "With the cauldron's power to span universes, our four friends could be almost anywhere."

"Who could have done this?" asked Jon Arbuckle, finally grasping the fact that something really, really bad had just happened.

"Who else?" said Garzooka through clenched teeth.

"*Vetvix!*" exclaimed the emperor, Garzooka, and Sorcerer Binky, all at the same time.

"Vetvix?" asked Jon Arbuckle. "Sounds like a cream you put on your cat when he has a rash."

"Oh, she's much more than a cream," replied the emperor. "Vetvix is an evil veterinarian. She uses dark magic to try to take over my universe. Her goal is to knock me off my throne."

"Maybe you could put a seat belt on your throne," suggested Jon Arbuckle. "Then she couldn't knock you off."

"What the emperor means," said Garzooka, "is that Vetvix uses her evil powers to try to get rid of Emperor Jon and make herself the ruler of this universe. If she ever took over the throne, we would all become victims of her horrible plan to create a universe of mindless mutants under her absolute control. She would combine humans and

27

animals into foul creatures who live for no other reason than to do her evil bidding. She must be stopped at all costs!"

"Oh," replied Jon Arbuckle. "That's bad."

Sorcerer Binky gazed into the cauldron. "It can only be Vetvix behind this," said the sorcerer. "No one else has the power to seize control of my cauldron."

Garzooka turned to Emperor Jon. "I've got to go after the others," said the Pet Force leader in a tense voice.

"But where will you begin?" asked the emperor.

"I'll program the *Lightspeed Lasagna* to start a search pattern on the widest possible setting," explained Garzooka. "I'll attempt to track the others using their life-sign signatures."

"I'm a Capricorn," said Jon Arbuckle. "And I think Nermal is a —"

"Not those signs," said Garzooka. "Each individual gives off a set of readings that is unique to his or her body. I will program my ship's computer for the readings of the missing Pet Forcers. With any luck, I will be led to them. I'll also search for Vetvix, since I believe if I find her, the others will be close by," concluded Garzooka.

"Good luck, Garzooka," said the emperor.

"Don't pick up any hitchhikers," added Sorcerer Binky.

"I hope you find the others, Garfield-in-a-weird-superhero-costume," said Jon Arbuckle. "My life would be very boring without my pets."

There is absolutely no way, in any universe, that your life could be any more boring than it already is, pets or no pets, thought Garzooka. Then he said aloud, "Please. Call me Garzooka."

Garzooka dashed from the throne room and practically flew down the spiral stone stairs that led to the palace garage. Finding the Pet Force ship, the *Lightspeed Lasagna,* he climbed inside and fired up the main engines. Then he punched the code into the remote control garage door opener and pushed the button.

The door rolled up slowly and the *Lightspeed Lasagna* pulled out of the garage. "Main thrusters to full," said Garzooka once the ship was outside.

Back in the emperor's throne room, the two Jons and the sorcerer heard Garzooka over the emperor's state-of-the-art communications panel.

As the *Lightspeed Lasagna* shot off into space, Garzooka heard Jon Arbuckle's voice saying, "Wow! This communications system is cool! Can you get cable on this thing?"

Garzooka shook his head, then switched off his speaker. He set up the ship's tracking equipment and started his mission to find his missing friends.

5

Meanwhile, Abnermal, Starlena, Odious, and Compooky tumbled out of control, through a dark, swirling tunnel.

Suddenly the spinning stopped. The four Pet Force members found themselves each standing on an individual platform. A fifth platform stood next to them, empty.

"Is everyone all right?" asked Starlena.

"My stomach's a little queasy," replied Abnermal, "but that could happen on a normal day just from listening to Garzooka talk."

"Speaking of Garzooka," said Starlena, concern showing in her voice, "where is he?" She instinctively assumed command of the Force in Garzooka's absence.

"Maybe he got sucked into the cauldron and was sent somewhere else," suggested Abnermal. "He could be in great danger!"

"He obviously was not transported here with us," said Compooky.

"But where are we?" Abnermal asked.

Starlena looked over at Odious. His head continued to roll around and around on his shoulders. Slobber flew in all directions.

"Odious!" shouted Starlena.

The shout startled the muscle-bound mutt. His head stopped rolling and his eyes focused on his teammates.

"Well, I don't know where we are, Abnermal," said Starlena. "But we are getting out of here." She tried to step off her platform and ran right into a powerful, invisible force field. "We're trapped!" she cried.

Starlena sang out her siren song, hoping its sonic force would break through the invisible wall. But the invisible wall kept the high-powered melody contained. The siren song bounced right back at Starlena, practically knocking her off her feet. "This wall is resistant to my sonic energy!" she exclaimed.

Abnermal tried next, sending out a dose of his freeze-power. His blast hit the force field and bounced back at him. In no time he was up to his waist in ice shards. "Looks like cold won't crack it, either!" he cried.

Odious smashed at the force field around him. Each time he pounded on the energy wall with his huge fists the wall stretched out, then snapped back into place with equal force, as if it were made of rubber. When the wall bounced back, the force hurled Odious to the floor of the platform. This didn't stop him from pounding the wall again and again, being thrown to the floor of the platform each time.

"I'm afraid these force fields are stronger than our powers," said Compooky.

"Where *are* we?" asked a frustrated Starlena. "And *who* is doing this to us?"

A low laugh filled the room. Then a tall, dark figure stepped from the shadows.

"Vetvix!" snarled Starlena.

The evil veterinarian stood before the heroes, hands on hips and head thrown back triumphantly. Her hideous laugh built to a shrill pitch that cut through the air and sent chills down Starlena's spine. "Welcome aboard my *Floating Fortress of Fear*," she cackled. Then she glanced around and the smile disappeared from her face. "But where is Garzooka?" she shrieked in distress. "Where is your portly leader?"

The four heroes glanced at the empty platform beside them. It was obviously meant for Garzooka, who had managed to resist the force of the cauldron twister.

Vetvix regained her composure. "His powers will be necessary for my ultimate goal of taking over the universe," she said calmly. "But for now, you four have more than enough power to begin my glorious crusade! Besides, knowing Garzooka as I do, I'm certain that he'll come looking for his

little lost teammates. And then *you* will help me capture *him!*"

"We'll *never* help you!" shouted Starlena.

"Soon you will be very glad to help me," replied Vetvix, laughing her horrible laugh. "You can't escape. You will never return to your own universe again."

A sudden look of shock came over the faces of Starlena and Abnermal. Odious continued to punch the force field and fall to the platform floor.

"Oh, yes," chortled Vetvix, noticing the expressions on the heroes' faces. "Don't look so surprised. I know all about your other universe — how you came through that sorcerer's cauldron to become Pet Force and save the day for your beloved Emperor Dumb. That is, Emperor Jon, of course. I know all about that."

Vetvix extended her arm, and a crystal ball floated down from above, landing gently in her outstretched hand. The crystal ball shimmered with radiant light. Within seconds the flickering shapes in the glittering orb sharpened and the Pet Force heroes could plainly see the image of Emperor Jon in his palace.

"I used my crystal ball to cast the spell that blocked your return to your own universe," explained Vetvix. "I brought you here because I need you for my next plan to conquer this universe. It is all coming together now."

What Vetvix did not know was one side effect of her portal-blocking spell: Jon Arbuckle accidentally getting pulled into her universe. At that moment, as she gazed into her crystal ball and peered at Emperor Jon, Jon Arbuckle was down on the throne room floor, busy counting the tiles. Therefore, Vetvix could not see Jon Arbuckle in her crystal ball image.

"Why are you telling us all this, Vetvix?" asked Starlena.

"It's very simple," replied the evil vet. "In a few moments you all will become the centerpiece of this plan."

"And what is this great plan you won't shut up about?" asked Abnermal.

"I'll ignore your pitiful insult," said Vetvix calmly, "for soon you will have no memory of ever having made it. In fact, you will have no memory at all! You see, I plan to create a being with incredible strength, a supercomputer brain, and amazing super powers. It will be my slave, and it will help me take over this universe!"

"And where are you going to get this super-powered being?" Abnermal asked, laughing at the plan, which sounded silly to him.

Vetvix pressed a button on the huge control panel before her. An enormous machine lowered ominously from the ceiling. "Why, from bits and pieces of the four of you!" she replied. Then her shrill laugh filled the room once again.

6

Back at Emperor Jon's palace, both the emperor and Jon Arbuckle paced back and forth across the throne room floor — which contained 1,927 tiles, as Jon Arbuckle proudly informed the emperor. Emperor Jon was fretting and worrying about the fate of Pet Force. Jon Arbuckle was still trying to understand the whole parallel universe thing, and exactly what had happened to him. Sorcerer Binky was using his cauldron to search for the missing heroes.

"So let me get this straight," said Jon Arbuckle as his pacing crisscrossed with the emperor's. "You are me, and I am you, but not really."

"As I far as I understand it," the emperor told him, "each person or animal in a universe has a parallel being in many other universes."

"What about plants?" asked Jon Arbuckle.

"I'm not sure," replied the emperor, his thoughts easily distracted. "I know I've never had luck with houseplants. They're always dying on me."

"I think you have to water them," said Jon Arbuckle, trying to sound as wise as he could.

"Anyway," continued the emperor, "Sorcerer Binky explained it to me. You and I are parallel beings, each from our own universe."

"Boy," said Jon Arbuckle. "More than one of me. If Garfield were here, he'd be so happy! Actually, I guess he is here, only he's not really Garfield — he's that Garzooka guy. How come when Garfield and the others came into this universe, they changed into Pet Force, but when I came in, I stayed me?"

"Garfield and the others replaced the original Pet Force," the emperor explained, "who are no longer in this universe. But because I am still here, you came through as you, not me."

The emperor's thoughts jumped back to the missing members of Pet Force. "How is your search going, Sorcerer Binky?"

"Oh, I get it," interrupted Jon Arbuckle. "Sorcerer Binky in this universe is the parallel being to Binky the Clown in my universe."

"You've got it, genius," replied the sorcerer, annoyed at once again being compared to a clown. Then he turned to the emperor. "No luck yet, your highness. But I'm still searching."

Emperor Jon shook his head. "I've never felt so helpless in all my time as emperor," he said sadly.

"How *did* you become emperor, anyway?" asked

Jon Arbuckle. "I know in my universe there's no royal blood in my family. Except for my uncle, who served as president of his bowling league for a while."

The emperor sat down on his throne. "Since there's nothing we can do until Sorcerer Binky or Garzooka locates the missing Pet Force members, I might as well pass the time and tell you the story."

Emperor Jon got comfortable and Jon Arbuckle settled into the plastic folding chair. Then the emperor began his story:

"When I was a little boy, growing up here on the planet Polyester, I took a job working in the emperor's palace. I worked as a servant to the emperor at that time, and he always treated me kindly. I worked very hard bringing him food, tidying up the palace, running errands into town — you know, that kind of thing.

"I soon became a trusted member of the emperor's court. I came to think of him like a favorite uncle. When I was seventeen, the emperor died suddenly. Everyone in the kingdom was very sad. The emperor had no children, and so the emperor's brother — his only living relative — was to become the new emperor."

"Excuse me," interrupted Jon Arbuckle. "Do you have any popcorn? I love popcorn with a good story."

Emperor Jon called for one of his servants to bring a tub of popcorn. Then he continued with his story.

"Where was I? Oh, yes! The emperor's brother was to become the new emperor, but he lived far away on a distant planet called Greps, and his journey to Polyester to claim the throne would take many weeks. And so, because I was a trusted servant for so many years, I was offered the crown until the brother arrived. Imagine that. Me, a teenage servant, becoming the emperor."

Sorcerer Binky leaned over to Jon Arbuckle and muttered quietly, "The emperor's brother had a much bigger head than the emperor and so a new crown had to be made. The advisers really offered Jon the old emperor's crown itself, as a memento, so he could remember the emperor he loved so dearly. They certainly were not offering him the emperorship, especially with the old emperor's brother on his way to claim the throne. After all these years, he still has no idea." Binky chuckled softly.

"What are you saying, Binky?" asked the emperor.

"Nothing, your highness," replied Binky nervously. "I was just asking our guest if he wanted more popcorn."

"I see," said Emperor Jon. He continued his tale. "Anyway, I got all choked up at the advisers' offer. 'You're offering me the crown?' I asked in disbelief.

"'Why not?' the top adviser replied. 'It fits, and besides, the emperor always liked you.'

"Well, I was beside myself with joy. They had offered me the crown. I was clearly now the acting emperor!"

Jon Arbuckle looked at the sorcerer, who simply rolled his eyes toward the heavens. "What happened to the emperor's brother?" he asked Emperor Jon, between the handfuls of popcorn he was stuffing into his mouth.

"He never showed," replied Emperor Jon. "Weeks slipped into months with no word from him. At the time we guessed that he had changed his mind about wanting to be ruler of the entire universe, or maybe he just got a better offer.

"Meanwhile, I had been acting as emperor, sitting on the throne, and everyone treated me like the boss."

"They were just humoring him until the brother arrived," whispered Binky.

"Finally, almost a year later, one of our scouting vessels found the remains of the emperor's brother's ship. We analyzed the ship's remains and our scientists concluded that the ship had run into a terrible meteor storm not far from Polyester. The ship was destroyed and the brother was killed.

"At that point my formal coronation ceremony was held, even though I had been emperor for almost a year. I've been emperor ever since."

By the time Emperor Jon finished his story, Jon Arbuckle was in tears. He realized that Emperor Jon came to power through a silly misunderstanding, but Jon Arbuckle was still a sucker for a happy ending.

"That's the most beautiful story I've ever heard," he sobbed, dabbing his eyes with a damp wad of popcorn.

All at once Sorcerer Binky shrieked. "*I've found them!*" he screeched, startling both Jons.

Emperor Jon and Jon Arbuckle rushed to the sorcerer's side. Peering over the cauldron's edge, they saw an image take form on the surface of the liquid. It was an image of Vetvix's *Floating Fortress of Fear*.

"It's Starlena, Abnermal, Odious, and Compooky!" cried the emperor. "And they're in big trouble!"

The two Jons and Sorceror Binky helplessly looked on as a horrible scene unfolded.

7

Inside the *Floating Fortress of Fear*, things had gone from bad to worse for Pet Force. Vetvix strapped the four Pet Force captives into her gruesome-looking machine. The horrible device now hummed with energy. Lights flashed, and power surges pushed the control meters to full power. Vetvix had perfected this machine during her many experiments in combining different animals. She had created an army of terrible mutant creatures, including a turtle-crow, a rabbit-frog, and her personal pet, Gorbull, who was half-gorilla and half-pit bull. This new, improved machine blended her magic with the latest in technology and could combine five creatures into one.

"In just a few short moments, Pet Force, as the universe has known it, will be no more," cackled Vetvix as the heroes struggled in vain to escape. "But don't worry, you won't feel a thing. And when my little experiment is over, I will at last have created a being powerful enough to begin my takeover of Emperor Jon's universe! Eventually I will need Garzooka's power as well, but for now, this will do nicely."

Vetvix threw the final switch on her dreadful device. Starlena, Odious, Abnermal, and Compooky all passed out. They dangled helplessly from the straps that held them. A few seconds later, a bizarre transformation took place.

Abnermal's hands separated from the rest of his body and floated toward the center of the machine. Starlena's head came off next and floated eerily in the air. The monitor attached to Compooky's head lifted off, taking with it his hyper-intelligent computer brain. Odious's head popped off, followed by his hands. Then his headless, handless body joined the pieces of his teammates floating in the center of the machine.

The body parts quickly formed into a bizarre combination of heads, hands, feet, arms, legs, and bodies. The Pet Forcers' body parts were all scrambled up! Then they broke apart and briskly re-formed into a different ridiculous combination. This happened several more times, until Vetvix adjusted the controls.

"It's such fun watching Pet Force fall to pieces," Vetvix said with a sigh. "But alas, it's time to take the machine off shuffle and program it to my precise specifications." When she had flipped the last switch on the control panel, Vetvix stepped back to watch the metamorphosis.

Slowly, Abnermal's hands attached themselves to the ends of Odious's muscular arms. Starlena's head lowered onto Odious's broad shoulders. Compooky's computer brain, complete with monitor, fastened on Odious's chest, its wires snaked into Starlena's head.

A loud buzzer sounded, indicating that the combination process was finally finished. Vetvix switched off the huge machine and quiet filled the room. Her strange creation stepped from the device and stood before her. This combination creature had the body and strength of Odious, the head and siren song of Starlena, and the hands, freeze-power, and force shield of Abnermal, all controlled by Compooky's hyper-intelligent computer brain — which had been reprogrammed during the transformation to obey only Vetvix!

"Step over here!" ordered Vetvix. The massive creature, still learning to walk in its new form, stumbled over to its new master.

"I am ready for my orders, master," the creature said in Starlena's voice, but in a dull, emotionless tone. All traces of the feisty Pet Force personalities were gone — wiped out. The creature had been completely brainwashed to be evil and follow Vetvix's commands without question. It still had Compooky's incredible brain, but its thoughts and actions were controlled by the evil veterinarian!

"How obedient you are!" said Vetvix, smiling. "I would like to test your powers. But first you need a name. Since you are my greatest mutant creation, and the first warrior who truly has the power to terminate Emperor Jon's rule of this universe, I will call you the *Mutanator*." The evil veterinarian then summoned a group of her mutant soldiers into the room.

"What do you need, O great and terrible Vetvix?" asked a half-cow/half-cheetah.

"Yeah, what can we do for you, your ultimate evilness?" asked a half-lizard/half-gerbil.

Vetvix ignored them. She turned instead to her new creature, the Mutanator. "Mutanator, focus your siren song on those soldiers."

The Mutanator instinctively knew how to use its awesome Pet Force powers. Without hesitation the Mutanator opened its mouth and out came Starlena's siren song. Vetvix covered her ears and watched as the hypnotic melody put the two mutant soldiers into a trance.

"Very good, Mutanator," said Vetvix. "Now, encase them in a prison of ice!"

The Mutanator shot Abnermal's freeze-power from its hands, instantly covering the unconscious soldiers with a thick, frosty layer of ice.

"Excellent!" cackled Vetvix. "Now, one final test. Mutanator, lift the combination machine over your head."

The Mutanator obeyed without emotion, without thought. It moved like an automated robot, blindly following Vetvix's every order. The Mutanator walked over to the massive combination machine, which weighed several tons. Even an elephant-ox — the strongest of Vetvix's mutant soldiers — couldn't budge it. The Mutanator grasped the machine and, flexing Odious's powerful muscles, easily lifted it into the air.

"Perfect!" purred Vetvix. "Now put it down — gently!"

The Mutanator placed the huge machine back onto the floor.

Vetvix gathered up the extra Pet Force pieces and placed them back into the force fields that had held them before the transformation. "I'll keep your leftovers handy for a future mutant creation," she said. "You just can't have too many body parts around in my business." Then she prepared to send the Mutanator on its first mission.

Vetvix flipped open the front of Compooky's monitor and went to work. "I have made a few final adjustments in the programming of your brain," she said when she had finished. "You are to proceed to the planet Armory, where Emperor Jon keeps his stockpile of weapons. That is where we will begin our attack. Once I control the weapons, you will proceed directly to the planet Polyester to lead my army in an assault on the emperor's palace!"

"Do you believe that I am strong enough to defeat the emperor's army?" asked the Mutanator, once Compooky's logical brain had analyzed the plan.

"Maybe not yet," replied Vetvix. "But by the time you are ready to attack Polyester, I plan to have Garzooka's power added to your own. Then no one will be able to stop us!"

Vetvix gave the Mutanator one of her fastest ships and was about to send it on its way. "Oh, one more thing," she said as the mutant creature prepared to leave. "I will control you and remain in constant communication through the monitor that is hooked up to your computer brain. I have connected your brain to the computer here in my fortress using a cellular remote."

She then switched on the monitor, and an image of her own face filled the screen. "It's true. You do look heavier on TV," she moaned, examining her face in the screen on the Mutanator's chest.

"Now go and do my bidding, Mutanator!" she shouted. "But know that I will be right there with you, keeping a close eye on your progress. Who says you can't be in two places at once?"

The Mutanator blasted off from the *Floating Fortress of Fear* in Vetvix's ship.

The evil veterinarian turned back to her lab. "I still have work to do," she muttered to herself as her mutant soldiers began to defrost and wake up. "When that do-gooder Pet Force leader Garzooka comes looking for his little lost friends, I'll have a lovely surprise waiting for him. Now that I control that teddy bear's computer brain, all his memories belong to me. When I scanned the brain, I learned everything there is to know about Garzooka, and Garfield — including the thing that scares him most!" Then she turned to an ancient book of evil spells and went about setting a trap for Garzooka, who was the universe's only hope.

8

On board the *Lightspeed Lasagna*, Garzooka grew more and more frustrated. He had been searching fruitlessly for his missing teammates and wasn't even close to finding them.

"Could they maybe make this universe a little bit *bigger*!" he muttered to himself as he scanned another quadrant for his friends' life signs. He was getting very cranky, as if the hugeness of the universe were a plot designed just to inconvenience him.

"So what if I never see those guys again?" he asked himself as he popped open another can of space rations and began to chow down hungrily. "I guess they *are* my friends, not to mention my superhero, crime-fighting partners. But if I have to live on this canned, mock-Spam space food for much longer, I'm going to consider going solo. How bad would that be? *The Adventures of Garzooka, Hero of the Universe!* That's a pretty good title for a book." Then he choked down another spoonful of his lunch.

"What I wouldn't give for a steaming tin of drippy, gooey lasagna," he moaned, making himself even hungrier.

All of a sudden a steaming tin of drippy, gooey lasagna appeared right before his eyes. Garzooka plucked it out of midair and stared at the delicacy before him. "Oh, great," he mumbled. "Now I'm hallucinating. I've definitely been out in space by myself for too long."

"You're not hallucinating, Garzooka," said a voice from the *Lightspeed Lasagna*'s communications system. It was Sorcerer Binky. "I sent that lasagna to you using an ancient spell I learned on the planet Parmesan," explained the sorcerer, "partly because I was sick of hearing you whining. But I also thought you should have a full stomach when I tell you that I've located Vetvix's *Floating Fortress of Fear!*"

"Let me get this straight," said Garzooka, completely ignoring the second, and most important, half of the sorcerer's message. "You have been able to magically send me lasagna all this time, yet you left me out here eating this mystery meat three times a day?"

"Did you hear what I said?" asked Sorcerer Binky. "I've found Vetvix's secret hideout!"

"I heard what you said," replied Garzooka. "You

could have been magically zapping me delicious meals all this time!"

"I wanted to make sure that when you rescued your teammates there was still some room in the *Lightspeed Lasagna* for someone other than you!" shot back Binky.

"Cute," said Garzooka, stuffing a huge slab of lasagna into his mouth. "Now, what about Vetvix?"

"I've located her *Floating Fortress of Fear* using my magic cauldron," repeated the sorcerer. "I'm transmitting the location to your ship's main computer now."

"Could you transmit a big tub of vanilla ice cream at the same time?" asked Garzooka.

"Don't press your luck," replied Sorcerer Binky.

"Garzooka, this is Emperor Jon. I understand things have been rough for you, but just think of your teammates!"

"Yes," added Jon Arbuckle. "Think of my poor lost pets!"

I'm trying not to, thought Garzooka, who at the moment was much more interested in the last remaining piece of lasagna that was calling out his name. He scarfed down the final piece, gave his belly a pat, then returned his mind to the problem at hand.

"I've got the coordinates, Emperor Jon," said Garzooka, throwing the *Lightspeed Lasagna* into top speed. "I'm on my way. Do you think you could send some more lasagna for my next meal in about — oh, fifteen minutes?"

"Find the others first," replied the emperor. "We'll talk about food later. Besides, I don't know what the big deal is with the canned rations. I happen to think they're delicious."

Just before Garzooka sped off, he heard Jon Arbuckle through the radio saying, "Really? Can I try some? Do you have an extra can around here?"

Garzooka shook his head. "I thought that *one* Jon was bad enough. I'd better put an end to this madness and get Jon Arbuckle back to his own dimension or this universe might not survive!"

Following the coordinates provided by Sorcerer Binky, the *Lightspeed Lasagna* soon arrived at Vetvix's *Floating Fortress of Fear*. Docking the ship, Garzooka ripped a hole in the locked door leading into the fortress with his razor-sharp right claw and slipped into the evil veterinarian's head-quarters.

Within minutes Garzooka had arrived at the door to her lab. "No time to be subtle," he cried, bashing the door right off its hinges with a power-ful blow from his fist. The steel door crumpled like a piece of paper and fell to the floor.

"Don't you superheroes ever knock?" said Vetvix calmly. She seemed to be expecting Garzooka's ar-rival.

Sprawled all over the lab, covering practically every square inch of the floor, were the blueprints for Vetvix's next evil creation. She put down the papers she was working on and turned her full at-tention to Garzooka.

"Where are my friends?" demanded the Pet Force leader.

"You have friends?" replied Vetvix sarcasti-cally. "That's the most shocking thing I've heard all day."

"You know what I mean, Vetvix!" shouted Gar-zooka. "Where are the others?"

"Oh, you mean the rest of the Pet Fools?" said Vetvix. "They're right over there." She pointed to the force fields that held the leftover pieces of Pet Force.

Garzooka was horrified to see Odious's head floating in midair, drooling. He saw Starlena's arms reaching up and touching her headless shoulders over and over, as if each time she expected her head to suddenly be where it wasn't a moment before. Compooky floated lifelessly within his force field, little more than a stuffed teddy bear now that his computer brain had been given to the Mutanator.

Abnermal, minus his hands, began chattering nonstop the moment he saw Garzooka. "Well, it's about time you showed," he whined at the Pet Force leader. "Where were you when she took us apart and made that monstrosity? Look, could you lend me a hand? Actually, two? She took my hands, and Starlena's head, and Compooky's brain, and Odious's body and made this — this thing called the Mutanator, and now it's taking over the universe. I'd give you a big hand, Mr. Superhero, but I'm a bit shorthanded right now. I need a handout."

Abnermal's pester-power had remained with his body, much to Vetvix's distress.

"This is the most wicked plan you've hatched yet, Vetvix," snarled Garzooka, "but I'm about to put an end to it. First I'll be taking my friends — or what's left of them — out of here. Then I'm going after this Mutanator character and somehow I'll figure out how to put all the pieces back in the right places."

"Nice speech, Garzooka," said Vetvix, "but you're forgetting one thing. I control Compooky's brain. I now know all there is to know about you, including what you fear the most — as Garzooka, and as Garfield the cat!"

Garzooka was shocked. *She knows my true identity*, he thought. *She must know all about me, not to mention all about the parallel universes!*

"I happen to know that Garfield the cat hates spiders," said Vetvix.

A shiver ran through Garzooka, as much from thinking about spiders as from realizing that Vetvix now knew his deepest, darkest secrets.

"And as Garzooka the superhero," Vetvix continued, "you still will be terrified of my giant space spiders!"

A trapdoor in the ceiling sprung open, and an enormous spider dropped to the floor. The spider was at least ten feet long, with huge, hairy legs. Its thick black body oozed a sticky white liquid. It was ready to spin its giant-sized web! Garzooka shrunk back in fear. *I hate spiders*, he thought. *Even little bitty ones. But this is ridiculous!*

Before Garzooka could move, four more giant spiders dropped from the ceiling. The enormous beasts surrounded the Pet Force leader, then began to close in.

9

A wave of fear and disgust swept over Garzooka. As Garfield, he hated spiders, even though he was bigger — much bigger — than they were. With the tables turned here, facing spiders that were almost twice his size, Garzooka swallowed hard and thought, *I wonder what's making me queasy — eating that mock-Spam, or the sight of these jumbo pests.*

Garzooka took a deep breath. *Boy, these guys smell bad!* he thought. Then he exhaled, spinning around on one foot, like a top. Gamma-radiated hairballs fired from his mouth, spraying in all directions.

The spiders raised their hairy legs, one by one, and batted the hairballs away like 65-mile-an-hour fastballs right down the middle of the plate. The hairballs hit the ground and fizzled out.

Okay, thought Garzooka, *I guess hairballs aren't going to do the trick. These guys are good. Very good!*

The circle of giant spiders continued to tighten, getting closer to Garzooka.

"How about a shave, you hairy vermin?" shouted Garzooka. He extended his razor-sharp right claw and leaped at the spider that was closest to him. The spider grabbed Garzooka between two of its legs and began to tighten its grip around his gut. "Can't breathe," moaned Garzooka. "Not that I mind missing out on the smell, but breathing is one of those things I really enjoy, like eating and napping. And defending the universe from evil creatures like you!"

Mustering all his strength, Garzooka jabbed his claw into one of the spider legs that held him. The spider chittered in pain and flung the hero away. He landed right at the foot of another spider.

Garzooka jumped up and smashed the spider with his powerful fist. But the huge creature responded by shooting a thread of incredibly thick webbing at Garzooka. Within seconds, the Pet Force leader was wrapped in a web cocoon, his arms pinned at his sides by hundreds of sticky threads.

Garzooka sliced upward with his claw, cutting himself free. He grabbed a spider by the leg, spun it around and around, then released it. The spider flew through the air, crashing into two others. The three startled spiders tumbled over each other, landing in a heap.

Energized by this small victory, Garzooka raced toward the remaining two spiders.

"Enough of this!" Vetvix shrieked at the spiders as she looked on. "Destroy him!"

From his prison, Abnermal continued to pester. "I'd lend you a hand, Garzooka," he called, "but I'm fresh out at the moment."

"Well, then, how about a little encouragement?" said Garzooka as he wrestled with the two spiders.

"Sure," replied Abnermal. Jumping up and down like a handless cheerleader, he chanted, "Garzooka, Garzooka, he's our cat, if he can't beat the giant spiders, it's probably because he's so fat!"

"Your confidence is touching," said Garzooka as he flipped one of the spiders onto its back.

"Hey!" shot back Abnermal. "What do you want from me? It rhymes!"

"So does *Abnermal, Abnermal, you're the best, the best at being a pestering pest!*" chanted Garzooka as the spider flipped him over and the second spider pounced onto his chest.

"Well, you'll never win any poetry contests, that's for sure," added Abnermal. "I'd beat you, hands down!"

"Right now, I'd settle for winning this battle against the spiders!" Garzooka grumbled, using all his strength to toss the spider off him.

As Garzooka battled the two spiders and Vetvix shouted words of support to the terrible creatures, the three other spiders were busy spinning a web. The three spiders worked as a team, weaving their sticky tapestry. The enormous web stretched from floor to ceiling and extended from wall to wall.

The two spiders battling Garzooka were simply buying time for their buddies. When they saw that the web across the room was complete, they rushed at Garzooka, slamming into him at the same time and sending him flying across the room. He landed smack in the center of the web, his back stuck to the sticky threads.

"Nice of you to stick around," quipped Vetvix as she rubbed her hands in cruel delight.

Garzooka strained to free himself. He pulled with his arms and legs but they didn't budge. Even his super strength was no match for this incredibly sticky trap. He opened his razor-sharp right claw, but he couldn't budge his arm enough to slice through the webbing. Garzooka was trapped.

Vetvix turned to the spiders, who were now baring their fangs. "And now, my hungry friends," she chortled, "the fly is caught in the web and the dinner bell is about to ring."

Garzooka watched as the spiders quickly closed in on him.

He looked around, panicking. He glanced down at the floor and spotted the mounds of blueprint paper that Vetvix had been looking at when he first came into her lab. A plan formed quickly in his mind.

Garzooka fired gamma-radiated hairballs into each corner of the lab. When the glowing hairballs hit the blueprints on the floor, the paper burst into flames.

Fire raced along the floor. The spiders all fled in fear, terrified of the fire.

"No!" shrieked Vetvix as she ran around the room stamping out the flames.

Garzooka spat another hairball at the webbing just above his right hand. The hairball melted through the strand of webbing, freeing his right arm. *That's just what I needed*, thought Garzooka.

Using his super-sharp claw, he slashed through the webbing, freeing first his left hand, then his legs, until finally his whole body was free. Dropping to the ground, he raced through the smoky lab toward the docking port containing the *Lightspeed Lasagna*.

"I'll be back when I have the rest of you guys," he shouted to what was left of his teammates.

"Hurry," called back Abnermal. "Get our real body parts back — I don't want any hand-me-downs."

Odious's head continued to slobber all over his force field prison. By this time, his head was bobbing up and down in a sea of drool.

Starlena's arms waved toward Garzooka, encouraging him to hurry.

Compooky floated lifelessly.

Vetvix was too busy putting out the flames, attempting to save what she could of her next evil plan, to try to stop Garzooka's escape. By the time she had put out the fire, the Pet Force leader was gone.

In the *Lightspeed Lasagna*, Garzooka blasted away from the *Floating Fortress of Fear*. "That was close," he said to Emperor Jon when he reported in a few minutes later. "One nice side effect, though," he told the emperor. "By setting those blueprints on fire, I not only managed to escape but I also destroyed the early stages of Vetvix's next nasty scheme — whatever it was — in the bargain."

"What about the pieces of the others?" asked the emperor.

"I think they'll be safe in those force fields until I return," explained Garzooka. "It would have done no good to have tried to take them with me. Right now I've got to capture the Mutanator and bring it back to the *Floating Fortress of Fear*. Only the machine that split our four friends apart can put them back together."

"I see, Garzooka," replied the emperor.

"You mean Abnermal is just as annoying with or without hands?" asked Jon Arbuckle, who had been listening as Garzooka briefed the emperor.

Garzooka ignored him.

"How do you intend to make Vetvix put the others back together once you've captured the Mutanator?" asked Emperor Jon.

"I haven't figured out that part yet," said Garzooka. "First things first. Now I must find the Mutanator!"

Then he slammed the ship into light speed and set off on his quest.

10

On board one of Vetvix's ships, the mighty Mutanator prepared for its first evil mission. Vetvix's face appeared on the Mutanator's monitor. She seemed upset and distracted as she finished cleaning up the mess left by the fire.

"We are approaching the planet Armory, master," the Mutanator reported in Starlena's voice.

"What?" she shrieked. "Oh, you. I almost forgot about you with the mess Garzooka made here. He scared off my giant spiders with fire, ruined my blueprints, and practically burned down my entire lab! I want you to capture Garzooka and bring him here. The best punishment I can think of would be to complete my original plan and put both of you into the combination machine to make him part of you. Then I'd get a more powerful Mutanator, and I'd be rid of that Pet Force pain in the neck at the same time."

"Should I set my sensors to find him, so we can crush the do-gooder now?" asked the Mutanator, growling. The creature was excited at the thought of a battle with Garzooka.

"No," replied Vetvix, now fully focused on the task at hand. "You are to carry out your main mission first. Garzooka will come to you soon enough. And when he does, you will bring him to me, and I will have my revenge."

"Very well, master," said the Mutanator. "Perhaps we should proceed right to the planet Polyester and take over the emperor's palace."

"You're the one with the supercomputer brain," snapped Vetvix. "You should understand military strategy. If we go right for the palace, we'll have to fight our way through all of the emperor's armies and weapons.

"So, my friend, you will start on the planet Armory, where the emperor stores the weapons for his army. When we have gained control of the weapons, the emperor's soldiers will be all but helpless. At that time we can begin our assault on the palace on Polyester. You will lead an army of my mutant soldiers, armed with the universe's finest weapons, and we will be unstoppable!"

The next day the Mutanator arrived at the planet Armory. Its ship orbited the planet just beyond sensor range.

"Transmit the codes," ordered Vetvix through Compooky's monitor.

Planet Armory had a complex security system. Secret password codes had to be sent to the planet below before any ship would be allowed to land. These codes, known only to Emperor Jon's top military staff — which, of course, included Pet Force — were stored in Compooky's memory. Now, of course, the Mutanator knew the codes, too.

"Transmitting now," said the Mutanator.

In the planet's control center, a technician received the signal and identified it as Pet Force's code. A few seconds later a voice came through the communications system on board the Mutanator's ship. "Your ship is cleared for landing, Pet Force," said the voice, "although I'm getting a strange reading on that ship. Its energy signature makes it out to be one of Vetvix's ships."

"That is correct," said the Mutanator in Starlena's voice. "The *Lightspeed Lasagna* required some repairs. We've been using this ship, which we recovered from Vetvix during our last battle with that vile veterinarian. Pet Force out."

"Vile veterinarian!" said Vetvix after the communication channel with Armory was closed. "You didn't have to lay it on that thick, you know. Next time just use my name!"

"I'm just going for realism here," said the Mutanator. Then it brought the ship down for landing.

When the Mutanator emerged from the ship, the guard at the weapons storage complex was stunned. He expected to see one of the Pet Force heroes. Instead, he was now face-to-face with

Vetvix's evil creation — a wicked combination of *four* Pet Force heroes.

"What in the world happened to you, Pet Force?" asked the guard.

"What's more important is what is about to happen to you!" screamed the Mutanator. It let loose with a freeze blast that encased the guard in a block of ice.

"Excellent start," mused Vetvix. "Now, into the storage complex!"

The Mutanator moved menacingly toward the enormous complex, which consisted of a series of buildings that held most of the weapons used by Emperor Jon's army. The mutant grabbed hold of the locked front door of the first building. "This door is nothing for a being with the strength of Odious!" it announced. It ripped the thick steel door from its hinges, tossing it aside like an old newspaper.

Panic swept through the complex. Guards rushed toward the bizarre creature that now strode into the heart of Emperor Jon's weapons stockpile.

Cries of "What is it?" "It's a monster!" and "Boy, Starlena's been working out!" spread through the complex.

"I will show you what I am," said the Mutanator calmly. Then it sang out with Starlena's siren song.

The soothing tune filled the building, and soon

everyone within earshot had fallen into a deep trance.

"I like this!" shouted Vetvix.

The Mutanator strolled through the complex, allowing Vetvix to view the vast supply of weapons that she now claimed as her own.

Suddenly a laser blast from the open doorway struck the Mutanator in the back. The powerful mutant went crashing into a stack of crates containing atomic detonators. Fortunately for everyone on the planet, they were not connected to any explosive devices.

The Mutanator got to its feet, shook off the blow, and turned to face its attackers. Several squadrons of soldiers had rushed to the complex in response to a distress message transmitted by the guards just before the Mutanator sent everyone off to nap time.

The Mutanator sang out again with Starlena's siren song, knocking out the first wave of soldiers and buying enough time to reach the doorway. Stepping outside, it saw wave after wave of soldiers rushing toward it.

"Your first real combat test, big guy," Vetvix said fondly.

"I am ready," the Mutanator rumbled. "Besides, I owe them one for that shot in the back."

The Mutanator reached out with Abnermal's hands and fired a huge sheet of ice from its fingertips onto the ground. The frozen sheet extended in

all directions. The soldiers that rushed the weapons complex slipped and tumbled, unable to find their footing.

Vetvix howled with laughter.

"Watch this," said the Mutanator.

As the soldiers tried in vain to get to their feet, the Mutanator leaped onto the side of the building and began to climb. Using the incredible strength of Odious, it carved out hand- and footholds, making its way to the roof.

When it reached the roof, the Mutanator ripped a huge, cone-shaped loudspeaker from the base into which it was bolted. The thick steel bolts, each one more than a foot long, snapped like toothpicks. The speaker was usually used to broadcast announcements to the troops. The Mutanator held the small end of the speaker up to its mouth and sang out loudly with Starlena's siren song.

The soldiers that had been trying to get to their feet now all crumpled to the ice in hypnotic trances.

The Mutanator tossed the speaker off the roof. It landed on the ground below. "I am the Mutanator!" it shouted, its muscular Odious arms raised triumphantly in the air. It was giddy with the feeling of experiencing its first victory. "I am the Mutanator!" it repeated, its clenched fists pumping in the air.

The Mutanator looked up from its perch on the roof and saw the skies above the planet Armory filled with a fleet of Vetvix's ships. Her army of mutant soldiers had arrived right on schedule. Vetvix smiled on the monitor screen. With the Mutanator in charge and a stockpile of the deadliest weapons in the universe now in her control, her plan seemed a certain success.

"We are now ready to begin our assault on the planet Polyester!" announced Vetvix.

"To the planet Polyester!" echoed the Mutanator. "And the end of Emperor Jon!"

11

Word of the takeover on Armory soon reached the emperor. The guards in the weapons complex had sent a video transmission off to the palace on Polyester at the first sign of attack. The monitor in the emperor's throne room now showed the scenes of destruction that had just taken place on Armory. Emperor Jon, Jon Arbuckle, and Sorcerer Binky also got their first look at the Mutanator.

"Looks like Starlena's been working out," said Jon Arbuckle as the three watched in horror.

"Either that or Odious is wearing much too much lipstick," added the emperor.

Sorcerer Binky tried to explain the concept of the Mutanator to the two Jons. The emperor then contacted Garzooka in the *Lightspeed Lasagna* and filled him in on the latest attack.

"So they hit Armory, eh?" muttered Garzooka over the emperor's communications system. "Very clever. Vetvix has always had the ships and the soldiers, and now she's got your weapons. It's a pretty good bet they're arming themselves for an attack on the palace."

Emperor Jon's face turned pale. There was no misunderstanding what Garzooka was saying, even for the emperor.

"Attack?" asked Jon Arbuckle, the panic showing in his voice. "Here? Are you sure you can't send me home yet?"

"Don't worry," said Garzooka, gritting his teeth and setting his course for the planet Armory. "I'll stop them. Garzooka out."

"Isn't there a plane I could catch or something?" whined Jon Arbuckle. He pulled out his wallet. "I have all the major credit cards, you know."

Emperor Jon put a reassuring hand onto Jon Arbuckle's shoulder. "Don't worry," said the emperor, hiding his own concern. "Garzooka has never let us down before."

But Jon Arbuckle *was* worried. In his mind the same terrifying thought kept rolling around and around. *Garzooka is really Garfield! Garzooka is really Garfield!*

12

Back on Armory, Vetvix's mutant soldiers were busy loading weapons into their ships. The Mutanator kept the guards and soldiers under control by alternately freezing them, putting them into trances, or sometimes simply pounding them.

A half-duck/half-cobra waddled over to the Mutanator, holding two different-sized laser rifles. "Which one should I take?" the creature asked the image of Vetvix in Compooky's monitor.

"Take them both," replied Vetvix. "After all, the price is right!"

Suddenly a deafening roar filled the skies above Armory. The *Lightspeed Lasagna* burst through the clouds and landed in a swirl of orange flames and dust. Garzooka leaped from the ship almost before it had hit the ground.

"What did I tell you?" Vetvix said to the Mutanator. "There was no need to search for Garzooka. I knew that in time the do-gooder would find you. Now take him prisoner and bring him

77

back to my *Floating Fortress of Fear,* where I will combine his strength with yours to make my Mutanator even more powerful. Then you can attack Polyester."

Garzooka looked over the damage that had been done on Armory. Then he stepped up to the Mutanator, who was standing in front of the entrance to the weapons complex. They stood face-to-face. "I am here to take you back to Vetvix," said the Pet Force leader.

"Funny," said the Mutanator. "I was just about to say the same thing."

Garzooka stared at the bizarre creature that was made up of parts of his four friends. The thought of battling this creature, no matter how evil it had become, left him with an uneasy feeling. *I've got to subdue the Mutanator without actually hurting it. Then I've got to bring it back to Vetvix so I can add it to the Pet Force pieces she's still holding and restore my friends to their normal — well, to their old selves.*

"Compooky," said Garzooka. "I know your brain is in there somewhere. What you are doing is wrong. It's evil. Come with me back to Vetvix's lab, where we can force her to make Pet Force whole again."

"A touching speech," said Vetvix from the monitor on the Mutanator's chest. "What do you think of it, Mutanator?"

"I think you are soft, Garzooka," said the Mutanator in a voice that sounded like Starlena's, but was cold and distant. "Because of that you will be easy to defeat!"

The Mutanator slammed Garzooka in the chest with its powerful fist. The Pet Force leader flew backward through the complex's opening and landed in the center of the weapons stockpile building. The Mutanator rushed into the building and leaped at Garzooka, who rolled away just in time. The Mutanator crashed to the ground.

Garzooka got to his feet in a flash. *I can't unleash my full power on the Mutanator*, he thought. *However evil it's become, it's still made up of pieces of my friends. I must defend myself, not to mention Emperor Jon's universe, but I don't want to hurt Starlena's head, or Abnermal's hands, or Odious's body, or Compooky's brain. If I can stun the Mutanator, then I can bring it back to Vetvix's lab and try to set things straight.*

Garzooka fired a gamma-radiated hairball at the Mutanator. He knew that Odious's body could stand the impact and not be badly hurt.

But the Mutanator put up Abnermal's shield before the hairball reached it. The glowing hairball bounced off the shield and went skittering across the floor, heading right for a pile of explosives.

The hairball hit the explosives and small rockets went flying everywhere. The rockets in turn crashed into other weapons, setting off a chain reaction. Explosions, fireballs, and laser blasts ricocheted around the complex.

Some of Vetvix's mutant soldiers rushed into the building at the sound of the explosions. "Get out!" shouted Vetvix. "This is just between the two of us. Well, the three of us, actually!"

Garzooka and the Mutanator now had to dodge exploding weapons as well as each other's fists. Garzooka sent a punch toward the Mutanator's midsection. The Mutanator blocked the blow and countered with a powerful kick that sent Garzooka crashing into a wall. It then fired a freeze blast that encased Garzooka in a solid block of ice.

"Load our frozen friend into the ship," ordered Vetvix, "and head back to my *Floating Fortress of Fear*."

As the Mutanator moved to obey, Garzooka sliced through the ice block with his razor-sharp right claw, shattering the frozen prison and freeing himself. Garzooka lifted the Mutanator over his head and tossed it into a pile of laser rifles.

"Don't count your Pet Force heroes until they hatch!" yelled Garzooka.

"Who's the birdbrain in this picture, Garzooka?" replied the Mutanator. "Not only do I have better powers and greater strength than you, but you just tossed me into a pile of top-notch weapons!" It aimed a laser rifle right at Garzooka.

Before the Mutanator could get a shot off, Garzooka fired a gamma-radiated hairball that struck the laser rifle, turning it into molten steel. Smoke rose from the Mutanator's charcoaled hands. It had to use its freeze-power to cool off its burning fingers.

Garzooka tackled the Mutanator, and the two rolled over and over on the ground, trading powerful punches and not-so-powerful insults.

"You've put on a bit of weight working solo," said the Mutanator as it pushed Garzooka off. "You must be eating the food rations for all five of us."

A roving grenade exploded above their heads. The walls and ceiling began to shake. The building was taking quite a beating from all the exploding weapons. Garzooka and the Mutanator kept on fighting.

"Any extra weight I've put on is pure muscle," said Garzooka through clenched teeth.

"The Mutanator's not talking about that ugly lump that sits on your shoulders!" added Vetvix.

"You stay out of this, Vetvix!" said Garzooka. "This is strictly a Pet Force matter."

The battle continued, as did the exploding of weapons. The walls and ceilings began to crack.

"Your unwillingness to destroy me has made you weak," said the Mutanator. Then it fired an ice boulder at Garzooka that knocked him to the ground. "It will be your undoing!"

The Mutanator sang out with Starlena's siren song.

"If you really have Compooky's brain, then you know better than that," said Garzooka. "You know that I'm immune to the siren song."

The Mutanator knew. But it also knew exactly what it was doing. The sonic shock waves from the powerful siren song were so loud that they shook the building. Using Compooky's computer brain to make a structural analysis, the Mutanator realized that the walls and ceiling had been weakened by the explosions that had been going off. The sonic power of the siren song was now enough to shatter the building's support.

Just then, the ceiling began to collapse, and the Mutanator threw up Abnermal's force field to protect itself. Huge chunks of the ceiling fell from above, burying Garzooka in a mountain of steel and plaster. The Pet Force leader was knocked out and lay unconscious. The battle was over, and the Mutanator had won.

13

The Mutanator carried Garzooka's unconscious body to its ship.

"Quickly, now!" ordered Vetvix. "To my *Floating Fortress of Fear*! I will add Garzooka's power to your own. Meanwhile, my soldiers will finish filling their ships with weapons here on Armory. They will await my signal to begin the attack on Polyester, which you — with Garzooka's added strength — will lead."

"Very good, master," replied the Mutanator as it piloted the ship away from Armory.

During the journey, Garzooka drifted in and out of consciousness. Images of the terrible fight he had just finished floated past him, mixed up with pieces of his Pet Force partners and several large pizzas to go — hold the anchovies. "Must stop Mutanator," he muttered in a weak voice. Then he passed out again.

When the ship arrived at the *Floating Fortress of Fear*, Garzooka was still not fully awake. The

Mutanator carried him to Vetvix's lab, where he was strapped into her combination machine. The Mutanator stepped into the machine next to him and Vetvix powered up the evil contraption.

"I will now combine Garzooka with my already mighty Mutanator and guarantee my victory over Emperor Jon!" screamed Vetvix. A horrible humming filled the lab. Lights flashed as the power surged through the machine's circuits.

"Hey, nice bit of rescuing, Garzooka," Abnermal shouted sarcastically from his force field prison near the machine.

Garzooka could barely hear his teammate's taunt over the noise from the combination machine, which grew louder and louder. It was at this moment that Garzooka was finally fully awake — just in time for the terrible realization that he was about to become part of the evil Mutanator!

Emperor Jon's palace . . .

Back at Emperor Jon's palace, the emperor, Jon Arbuckle, and Sorcerer Binky were gathered around the cauldron, watching this awful scene take place.

"Is there nothing we can do?" asked the emperor desperately.

"I'm afraid not," replied the sorcerer.

"Then this truly is the end of Pet Force," said the emperor sadly. "Soon Vetvix will attack the palace, my reign as emperor will be over, and peace in this universe will be no more. Dark days will follow as Vetvix creates a universe of mindless mutants under her absolute control — foul creatures who live for no other reason than to do her evil bidding."

Jon Arbuckle still didn't grasp the meaning of the situation. He didn't realize the impact that the end of Pet Force would have on Emperor Jon's universe. He now leaned over the edge of the cauldron and stared at the events unfolding in Vetvix's lab. "So you mean this is happening right now, in another place, but we can see it here in the magic cauldron?" he asked for the fourth time.

The sorcerer, who was too distressed at the current situation to muster a snappy answer, simply nodded.

"Wow!" said Jon Arbuckle. "It's kind of like TV, only rounder."

The emperor ignored him and spoke to Sorcerer Binky. "With all of Pet Force trapped, what we need is another hero to step up and save the day — but, of course, that was always Pet Force's job. Who can do that now? Who can be the hero we need?"

Jon Arbuckle stood up on his toes and leaned farther over the cauldron to get a better view. "You guys wouldn't have any more popcorn, would you?" he asked. Then, all at once, he lost his balance and fell into the cauldron.

Jon Arbuckle didn't know what was happening to him. He tumbled through a dark void, spinning head over feet, around and around. *Maybe this cauldron thing is like a 3-D television, where I'm part of the action*, he thought, trying to make sense of what was happening. *Gee, if that's true, I hope it doesn't pick up any nature shows with hungry lions or packs of hyenas.*

What Jon didn't realize was that he was about to tumble right into the lab aboard Vetvix's *Floating Fortress of Fear*! The same spell that had pulled Starlena, Abnermal, Compooky, and Odious through the cauldron and into the lab earlier had now also sucked in Jon.

Dropping out of thin air, Jon landed right on top of Vetvix just as she was about to throw the final switch to combine Garzooka with the Mutanator.

"What is this?" shrieked Vetvix as Jon crashed into her. They were both knocked out by the impact.

The force of Jon landing on top of her threw Vetvix's arm against the *reverse* lever on her combination machine. The machine shut down, then started up again. But instead of combining Garzooka with the Mutanator, the machine, now in reverse, began to break the Mutanator apart. Within seconds, the evil mutant had been broken into the pieces of the individual Pet Force members.

Nice work, Jon! thought Garzooka. *Pretty heroic, for a world-class nerd!* Energized by the turn of events, Garzooka flexed his mighty muscles. One by one, the straps that held his arms, legs, and chest burst open.

With the power still humming and Vetvix still stunned, Garzooka leaped from the machine. He ran to the control panel and cut off the energy in the force field prisons. With the force fields down, he quickly grabbed the remaining pieces of Pet Force and placed them gently into the machine.

Garzooka watched as the pieces of the four Pet Force heroes whirled around inside the machine and began to reform. Heads, hands, and brains joined with bodies in a flash. When the process was complete, the machine shut down and the room grew quiet.

Only something was very wrong!

Abnermal's head was on Starlena's body, with Odious's legs. Starlena's head was on Abnermal's body, with Odious's arms. Compooky's head was attached to Odious's body, which was attached to Starlena's legs. And Odious's head was connected to Compooky's body.

"Get those big, burly arms off my body right now," shouted Abnermal's head. "I look like a gorilla."

"You think you've got problems," shot back Starlena. "I'm the one stuck like this. Your puny body can hardly hold my head up."

Meanwhile, Compooky's body floated around the combination machine, and Odious drooled all over the mixed-up Pet Forcers.

"There is a bright side to all this," said Compooky.

Everyone turned, then burst out laughing at the sight of Compooky's teddy bear head on Odious's massive, muscular body.

"When the machine split us apart again, my brain returned to normal," continued Compooky, ignoring the laughter of his teammates. "Now all of Vetvix's evil programming is gone."

"Compooky looks good with muscles," said Abnermal's head. "Maybe we should leave him the way he is!"

Odious's arms, attached to Abnermal's body, lifted Starlena's head. The head balanced for a moment, then toppled over in the other direction.

At that moment, both Vetvix and Jon Arbuckle woke up. Vetvix stared at Jon Arbuckle, thinking that he was Emperor Jon!

"Well, isn't this convenient?" she said, sneering at the sight of the emperor right within her grasp. "Emperor Jon here in my *Floating Fortress of Fear*. No need to go all the way to Polyester to capture you. You've been delivered right to my door. I'll admit you look strange without your royal robes and crown. But there is no doubt you are the real thing, the big prize, the emperor I've been pursuing for so long. What have you got to say now?"

"Have you got anything to eat around here?" replied Jon. "I'm starving. You know, a tuna casserole, peanut butter and jelly, or maybe a marshmallow treat or two?"

Vetvix was stunned into silence by this response.

Meanwhile, during Vetvix's brief conversation with Jon, Garzooka had snuck around behind her. While Vetix was distracted by the man she assumed was the emperor, Garzooka fired a gamma-radiated hairball at her. He managed to catch the evil veterinarian with her guard down. The hair-ball struck Vetvix and exploded in a burst of radioactive power. Vetvix crumbled to the floor, unconscious.

"All right, everyone!" Garzooka ordered. "Let's try this again!"

Garzooka searched for the machine's original setting — the setting from the first time Vetvix scrambled up Pet Force. When he found it, he powered up the machine and hoped for the best.

Once again, the four Pet Force heroes broke apart. Odious's head banged into Abnermal's as it crisscrossed, heading for its correct body.

"Hey!" shouted Abnermal's head. "Watch where you're going!"

"Oh, leave him alone," scolded Starlena's head as it detached from the annoying kitten's body. "You can have your oversized arms back," she added as Odious's head drifted past her.

When the process ended, Pet Force had been restored. The four heroes stepped from the machine, flexed fists and muscles, tested powers, and got reunited with their own selves.

"What about Vetvix?" asked Starlena.

"I suggest we place her into one of these force field prisons before she awakens," said Compooky.

"Good idea," said Garzooka. "But first . . ."

Garzooka placed Vetvix into the combination chamber. Then he turned on the machine. "I think she'd be a lot less trouble to us in the future in four or five pieces," he said as the machine built to a loud hum.

Suddenly two of Vetvix's mutant soldiers burst into the room. The half-cow, half-cheetah and the half-lizard, half-gerbil dashed toward the combination machine. Their blind loyalty to Vetvix had been programmed into their brains at the time she had created them, and they rushed to her rescue.

"Master!" cried the half-cow, half-cheetah. "I must save my master!"

"I'm coming, Vetvix!" yelled the half-lizard, half-gerbil.

The two mutant creatures jumped into the combination machine just as it reached full power. Pet Force looked on in amazement as first Vetvix, then the two mutant soldiers broke apart. Arms, legs, bodies, and heads floated through the air, then re-formed in new, bizarre combinations. In the middle of this process, Vetvix woke up.

"*No!*" she shrieked, but she was powerless. Once the process had begun, there was no stopping it, and with her body all in pieces, her magic had left her as well.

The machine finished its gruesome task. Vetvix's arms were now attached to the cow's body. It trotted out of the lab. The cheetah's head rested on Vetvix's shoulders, which were attached to the gerbil's legs; this distorted creature crawled away, growling. Vetix's legs now extended from the gerbil's head. They ran around and around in circles, powered only by the gerbil's tiny brain.

As for Vetvix's head, it was now attached to the lizard's body. "I will get you for this, Pet Force!" she shrieked. "Right now!" Her brain tried to control the lizard's body, but she wasn't used to her new limbs and the signals got crossed. The Vetvix-lizard stumbled around the room, bumping into walls and tripping over wires.

While Vetvix raved about her upcoming revenge, Compooky called out to Garzooka. "It was Vetvix's crystal ball that blocked the dimensional portal and prevented us from returning to our own dimension," the cyberbear informed the Pet Force leader.

The sparkling orb now hovered above the combination machine.

"I can take care of that right now," announced the Pet Force leader. He climbed onto the combination machine.

"Leave that alone!" shouted Vetvix.

"Or what?" taunted Garzooka. "You'll shed a layer of skin on me?"

Garzooka snatched the crystal ball out of the air like a power forward snagging a one-handed rebound. Returning to the ground, he crushed the crystal between his palms. Sickly green smoke and a foul stench filled the room.

"No!" shrieked Vetvix. "My magic!"

By the time Garzooka had finished grinding the crystal into tiny pieces, the smoke had cleared, and the magic in the crystal was gone.

"One more task remains," said Garzooka. "We must return to the planet Armory and undo the damage you did as the Mutanator. Vetvix's army is still preparing to attack the palace."

Then he turned to the Vetvix-lizard. "I guess *you* won't be giving us any more trouble, lizard-legs," said Garzooka.

"You wait right there, fat cat," snarled the Vetvix-lizard. "I'll teach you a lesson!" Again Vetvix set out after Garzooka, and again she could not control the lizard's body that now held her head. She crashed into a chair, then fell in a heap.

Garzooka picked up the unconscious Vetvix-lizard and placed it into a force field prison. Compooky flipped the power on, and an energy wall formed, trapping the Vetvix-lizard inside.

The last few remaining mutant soldiers in the *Floating Fortress of Fear* raced into the lab and rushed toward Pet Force out of blind loyalty to Vetvix. Abnermal and Starlena easily neutralized their attacks using his freeze-power and her siren song.

"Excuse me," said Jon Arbuckle as Pet Force headed out of the lab. Garzooka had forgotten about him in all the excitement. Jon was, of course, terribly confused by all he had just seen. However, he was able to formulate one question. "Does all this mean we can go home now?" he asked.

"Yes," replied Garzooka. "After we clean up a little unfinished business."

As they left the lab, Compooky scrambled the entry code so that Vetvix's soldiers couldn't get in to rescue her. Then Garzooka led the others to the *Lightspeed Lasagna.*

14

On board the *Lightspeed Lasagna*, Pet Force, reunited and back at full strength, settled in for the trip to Armory.

"Welcome back, guys," said Garzooka as he punched in the course. He had just finished telling the others his view of what had happened while they were under Vetvix's spell. "It's much nicer being on the same side. Although I could easily have defeated you, if I wasn't concerned about hurting you."

"Oh, yeah?" said Abnermal, taking up the challenge. "What makes you think *we* weren't taking it easy on *you*?"

"Ah, the peaceful sound of brotherhood and teamwork aboard the *Lightspeed Lasagna*," said Starlena sarcastically. "It's great to have things back to normal." Then she added under her breath, "We could have beaten you in a heartbeat if we'd wanted to."

Garzooka shot her a glance. Then he turned to Compooky. "How is Odious holding up?" asked the Pet Force leader. "It was his body that took the brunt of my attack."

Compooky did a quick medical scan of Odious. "My readings indicate that physically, he's just fine," reported Compooky, glad to once again be in charge of his computer brain. "As for mentally . . ."

Odious was busy batting dust balls from one side of the ship to the other — and keeping score.

"No change there," said Garzooka.

During this conversation, Jon Arbuckle was busy exploring the cockpit of the *Lightspeed Lasagna*.

"Wow!" he said for about the hundredth time since arriving in this universe. "What a neat ship! What does this do?" he asked, reaching for a button on the ship's control panel.

"Don't touch that, whatever you do!" Garzooka quickly pushed Jon's hand away.

"Why not?" asked Jon, getting curious and excited. "Does it set off some thermonuclear radiation bomb that would fry half the universe?"

"No," replied Garzooka. "It defrosts the food storage freezer, and I've still got a piece or two of leftover lasagna in there."

"Speaking of food," said Jon, "what have you got to eat on this ship?"

Garzooka smiled and handed Jon a can of mock-Spam space food. Jon gobbled it down hungrily. "Dee-licious!" he exclaimed. "May I have another, please?"

The planet Armory . . .

On the planet Armory, the captain of Vetvix's mutant soldiers was growing impatient. "There's got to be something wrong," he said to his lieutenant. "We should have received Vetvix's signal to head for Polyester by now."

Suddenly the *Lightspeed Lasagna* roared down from the sky above, its front lasers blasting.

"It's Pet Force!" shouted the captain as his troops scattered, running for cover.

The *Lightspeed Lasagna* landed and Pet Force leaped from the cockpit.

"Let the fur fly!" they all shouted as they rushed into action.

Odious interlocked his fingers and gave Starlena a two-handed boost. Up she floated, extending the arms of her costume to catch an updraft of wind. She glided gracefully to the roof of the weapons complex.

Meanwhile, Garzooka picked up the loudspeaker that the Mutanator had used earlier. He handed the speaker to Odious, who climbed up the side of the building to bring it to Starlena.

When Odious reached the roof, he spotted two

mutant soldiers sneaking up behind Starlena. Firing his super-stretchy stun tongue, he scrambled the brains of first one, then the other. Then he handed the speaker to his teammate.

Starlena put her mouth to the small end of the speaker and sang out with her siren song. Throughout the complex, Vetvix's mutant soldiers fell into hypnotic trances.

Compooky and Abnermal went from ship to ship in Vetvix's fleet. The ships were filled with the emperor's weapons.

Abnermal fired freeze blasts at the hulls of half the ships. The incredibly cold temperatures caused the metal of the ship construction to shatter like glass. Compooky reprogrammed the computers on the other half so that it would take even the finest computer technicians in the universe days — not counting the time spent on hold on the tech-support line — to get them working again.

The leader of the emperor's guards thanked Pet Force, then ordered his guards to bring the weapons from Vetvix's disabled ships back into the storage complex. Work also began on repairing the building that was destroyed during Garzooka's battle with the Mutanator.

Pet Force and Jon Arbuckle then returned to the emperor's palace, where they were greeted by an extremely happy Emperor Jon and Sorcerer Binky.

"Well done, Pet Force," said the emperor. "I

don't think Vetvix will be bothering us again. And well done to you, too, Jon Arbuckle. As it turns out, you were the surprise hero I was hoping for. Your brave act of diving into the cauldron saved my universe."

"But I —" began Jon Arbuckle, starting to explain that his falling into the cauldron was simply an accident.

"No, no," interrupted the emperor. "No false modesty. I believe in giving credit where credit is due!"

Jon Arbuckle shrugged. "Thank you, your highness," he said, bowing. As he bent over, his pants split right up the seam.

"It seems we have more in common than just our uncanny good looks," said the emperor with a smile.

"I guess we both need a good tailor now," replied Jon Arbuckle. "Well, this is certainly an adventure I'll never forget," he continued, shaking hands with the emperor and Sorcerer Binky. "After all, how many people get to meet their exact doubles in an alternate universe?"

"Are you ready to return home?" asked the sorcerer.

Jon Arbuckle nodded. Pet Force stepped up behind him.

Then Sorcerer Binky began chanting:

*"We've had some fun,
a laugh, a chortle.
Now send them home,
right through the portal!"*

The liquid in his cauldron began to swirl. In a
blinding flash, Pet Force and Jon Arbuckle disappeared into the dimensional portal.

"He's right, you know," said the emperor after
the six were gone. "It's not often that you get to
meet your exact double from an alternate universe. One thing's for sure: He'll never forget this
experience." Then the emperor smiled and patted
his old friend the sorcerer on the back.

15

Our universe, Jon Arbuckle's living room . . .

*Z*AP! Garfield, Odie, Arlene, Nermal, Pooky, and Jon Arbuckle were transported through the dimensional portal. They came through the cover of *Pet Force* #100 and landed in Jon Arbuckle's living room.

Jon was confused and disoriented (even more than usual). He had a vague recollection of having just had a strange experience, but he couldn't quite put his finger on it, just as the five Pet Force members were not quite sure if *their* first adventure had been real or just a dream. Jon now sifted through the fading memories of super powers, cauldrons, headless bodies, and a very lovely plastic folding chair.

Jon glanced around the room at the others, but the five friends offered no clue as to whether or not his memories were real. Everyone seemed to be doing something perfectly normal — for them, at least!

Garfield alternated between bites of lasagna and two-minute naps, with Pooky faithfully beside him. Nermal had his nose buried in a comic book. Arlene casually flipped through the pages of a magazine. Odious trotted back and forth in front of Garfield, looking at his lasagna and creating a pool of drool in the carpet.

That evening, Jon and the others were huddled on the couch, watching one of Jon's favorite TV shows, *The Adventures of the Fantastically Phenomenal Five* — the story of a team of five superpowered friends who battled evil and saved the day once a week. Between fistfuls of popcorn, something stirred in Jon's memory. *Superheroes*, he thought. Then he turned to the others.

"You know, maybe *you* guys should form a superhero team," he suggested.

Garfield looked at the others, wondering if Jon was beginning to recall his adventure in the parallel universe.

Jon mulled this thought over for a moment, looked at the pets again, then burst out laughing!